To

_____

_____

From

_____

_____

To Ferdinand   M.M.
For Mr Trellis   A.H.

Text copyright © 2011 Margaret McAllister
Illustrations copyright © 2011 Amanda Hall
This edition copyright © 2011 Lion Hudson

The moral rights of the author and illustrator
have been asserted

A Lion Children's Book
an imprint of
Lion Hudson plc
Wilkinson House, Jordan Hill Road,
Oxford OX2 8DR, England
www.lionhudson.com
ISBN 978 0 7459 6200 9

First edition 2011
1 3 5 7 9 10 8 6 4 2

A catalogue record for this book is available
from the British Library

Typeset in 15/20 Lapidary 333 BT
Printed in China July 2012 (manufacturer LH17)

Distributed by:
UK: Marston Book Services Ltd, PO Box 269, Abingdon, Oxon OX14 4YN
USA: Trafalgar Square Publishing, 814 N Franklin Street, Chicago, IL 60610
USA Christian Market: Kregel Publications, PO Box 2607, Grand Rapids, MI 49501

The Lion Classic
Aesop's Fables

MARGARET MCALLISTER

Illustrated by AMANDA HALL

CONTENTS

CONTENTS

THE LION AND THE MOUSE

A VERY TINY MOUSE ran over a hill and down the other side and… HELP!

It wasn't a hill at all. It was the head of a sleeping lion – and if the mouse had known that, she would have gone round the long way. But she hadn't known anything about the lion until it woke up and trapped her little tail under its huge paw. When she looked up, trembling, she saw the lion's great white teeth and his wide red mouth ready to swallow her.

"Oh, ple–ple–please!" squeaked the mouse. "Please, sir, let me go! I'm so small, I'm not worth eating! You won't like me! Oh, please, sir, I didn't mean to wake you up! Please, please, pardon me and let me go and I promise, sir, I promise on my mother's tail that I'll do you a big favour if ever I can!"

Fortunately for her, the lion was in a good mood. The idea that this tiny mouse could ever do him a favour was so funny that he didn't have the heart to harm her.

"I'll look forward to that," he said. "Off you go!" He lifted his paw, and the mouse squeaked a thank you before darting into the bushes and hiding before the lion could change his mind.

It was some time later that the hunters came to the forest, hoping to trap a lion to take home as a gift to the king. They hung up a net, disguised it with leaves and branches, and hid among the trees, waiting for a lion to stalk past that way.

The lion came prowling slowly through the forest. The minute he stepped onto that net, the men pulled it tight, tied it up, and came to admire their catch.

They were impressed by the size of the lion and congratulated each other on catching such a large, strong animal. He was too big to carry or drag back to their cart, which was at their camp, so they decided to bring the cart to the lion instead. They weren't worried about leaving him where he was, because, as they said, he couldn't run away. Still proud of their own cleverness and wondering how much the king would pay them for such a magnificent lion, they went away to bring back their cart.

They didn't know about the little mouse, hiding in a hole in a tree trunk, watching. The lion didn't know she was there either, but ever since the day when he had spared her life, she had stayed close to him, watching for the time when he might need her help. The minute the hunters were out of the way, she ran to the lion as he lay growling with pain and anger.

"Keep still, sir," she said. "I'll start with this rope across your shoulder, because it seems to be hurting you." Quickly, she gnawed through the rope, then scampered across to his face.

"Excuse me, sir," she said. "If I can get through the rope across your mouth, you can help to free yourself." She knew that the lion was a noble beast who had let her go before and would not hurt her now. Between them, they bit through all the cords until the lion was free.

"You see!" she said. "I told you I'd do you a favour one day!" And she ran away.

The hunters came back to find the empty net, the bitten ropes, and some flattened grass where the lion had been. That was the only trace of the lion, and so they all blamed each other for letting him get away, argued, and went home grumbling. None of them saw a bright-eyed little mouse watching from a tree trunk!

SMALL FRIENDS MAY BE
GREAT FRIENDS.

THE HARE AND THE
TORTOISE

EARLY MORNING WAS Exercise Time in the forest. Rabbits jumped in and out of their warrens, moles ran round and round their tunnels, and squirrels raced up and down trees (but squirrels do that anyway). None of this was enough for Hare. Hare did a few stretches, ran all the way around the forest three times, did ten sit-ups, a sprint, twenty star jumps, running on the spot, one more circuit of the forest, and some stretching. While he did all that, Tortoise crawled around a tree and ate a dandelion.

When Hare had finished his exercises, he sprawled on the grass. The squirrels and rabbits and a hedgehog or two had been watching him, so he couldn't resist bragging.

"There's nothing like a good run in the morning, is there?"

he said. "Mind you, I'm not as fit as I should be. It took me twenty seconds to do the sprint this morning and I'm aiming to do it in fifteen. Maybe I should train for a marathon this year. What do you think?"

The squirrels shrugged. They didn't care. The rabbits whispered to each other. Tortoise finished his dandelion. Hare sauntered over to him.

"Poor old Tortoise," he said. "Don't you ever wish you could run? Have you ever tried?" He laughed, and patted Tortoise's shell in an annoying way. "It took you all morning just to plod around that tree."

Tortoise turned his head slowly, stretching his wrinkly old neck to look up at Hare. Then without a word he crawled a few paces forward and started on another dandelion.

Hare laughed loudly and looked around to see if the other animals were laughing too. Some of them were grinning a bit, but that was all.

"Never mind, Slow-Go," said Hare. "I won't challenge you to a race!" He seemed to think this so funny that he had to lie on his back laughing and kicking his legs in the air.

However, when he got up again, the tortoise said mildly, "Won't you? I don't mind. I'll race you if you like."

Hare was so astonished that he forgot to laugh. He even forgot to close his mouth and stood there staring, with one ear up and the other ear down.

"We'll start from this tree," said Tortoise. "We'll take the right-hand path through the forest to the bridge, then cross over, turn left, and go straight along the river bank to Owl's

Oak Tree. That will be the finishing post. Shall we start at midday tomorrow?"

"Midday!" exclaimed Hare. "You'll never finish it before dark, and we'd have to send out search parties for you! We'll start at nine o'clock – do you think you can get here by nine?"

Tortoise slowly nodded his wise, crinkled old head, and ate another dandelion.

At nine o'clock, Tortoise was waiting at the starting line. Hare arrived, jogging, and did a few warm-up exercises. A hedgehog read out the rules – "No pushing, no tripping up, no cheating, and no jumping over your opponent" – and blew the whistle.

Tortoise moved steadily off. Hare let him get a start. All the other animals thought that this was very gracious of him, until he ran after Tortoise and crawled slowly along behind him, turning his head slowly from side to side as Tortoise did. Then he laughed, ran around Tortoise, and had soon sprinted out of sight.

Before long, he was far ahead and deep in the forest – so far ahead that he couldn't see the spectators any more, so he had nobody to show off to. He stopped, did a few stretches, walked down to the stream for a drink, and found a quiet pool where he could check his reflection. He was so pleased at what he saw that he stopped for a while to preen his ears and admire the handsome animal smiling smugly back up at him, until a duck landed on the water and spoiled it.

Still, there was no hurry. Hare walked the next bit, stopped to eat some clover, and ran as

far as the bridge. It was a beautiful sunny morning and
a few pretty female hares were dabbling their paws
in the river, so he stopped to lean on the wall of the
bridge for a while and look down at the water, hoping the girls
would talk to him. They didn't, so at last he stretched and said,
"Suppose I should get on. I'm in a race." He winked at them.
"No rush! I'm way ahead!" And he jogged gently on as if he had
all the time in the world.

All that standing in the sun at the bridge had given him a
headache. What he needed was a little snooze, and there was
plenty of time for that. Hare settled his back against a tree root,
folded his paws, and drifted into a doze. When he woke
up there was still no sign of Tortoise, so he did a few
running-on-the-spot exercises and ran on again.

As he drew near Owl's Oak Tree, he could
hear the excited voices of animals.

They must have gathered at the tree to welcome the victorious Hare! (Oh, and to wait for poor old Tortoise.) He ran on, waving with both front paws as he came in sight of the tree. He took a deep breath and opened his mouth to shout, "Hi, everyone!" and show that he wasn't out of breath – but then he stopped in astonishment and couldn't say anything at all.

Hare couldn't believe what he was seeing! He shut his eyes and opened them again, but it was still there.

THE TORTOISE WAS IN FRONT OF HIM!

HOW DID THAT HAPPEN?

Tortoise must have crawled past him while he was asleep! That wasn't fair! He galloped toward the oak tree, knowing that he had to win, but he was too far behind. To the cheering of the animals, Tortoise crawled to the tree, nodded his head, and turned slowly around, waiting to shake paws with Hare. While he was waiting…

… he ate a dandelion.

SLOW AND STEADY WINS THE RACE.

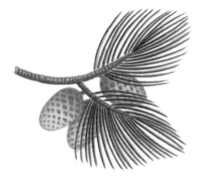

THE FROGS WHO
ASKED FOR A KING

THE FROGS WERE no trouble at all. They hopped in and out of swamps, croaked a lot, and ate flies. They rarely argued, or if they did, they soon forgot what they were arguing about and couldn't be bothered to fight about it (whatever it was), and went back to croaking and eating flies. They were no bother at all to anyone (except the flies).

BUT…

One lazy, sunny afternoon, the frogs began to talk about kings. Somebody pointed out that the lion was the king of the beasts, but the frogs all agreed that they weren't beasts at all. They were amphibians, and amphibians didn't count.

"Does that mean," asked a fat green frog, "that we don't have a king?"

"I suppose it does," said another. "That's not fair."

"No, it isn't," said the fat green frog. "Everybody else has a king. If we had a king, he'd tell us what to do."

"And he'd make sure that we did it," said another. "We'd be organized."

"That's what we need," said a young frog as it plopped out of the mud. "Someone to be our leader and tell us what to do. No frog was ever famous, was it? No frog was ever important! There are no hero frogs in the old stories! The most exciting thing we ever do is croak about in the swamp! If we had a king, he'd get us doing… doing… er…"

"Something else!" said the fat green frog.

"Exactly!" said the young frog. "He'd get us doing something that isn't croaking in the swamp!"

The frogs held a meeting. After a lot of croaking, they decided to call out to their god, whose name was Jove, and ask him if they could have a king.

Jove pretended to take them seriously, but secretly he found this very funny. He didn't know what the silly frogs would do with a king, but he agreed to send them one. He threw a log into the swamp, and wondered what they'd think of that.

The log fell into the swamp with such a splash that all the frogs leaped out and hid under stones. An elderly frog fainted.

"What a great king!" whispered the frogs from their hiding places. "Isn't he terrifying! Isn't he powerful!"

When they had watched for a long time from a safe distance, they realized that the log didn't do anything. When they called out "Crrk!" and "Croak–k–k" and "Oh, Great Majesty, would

you like a fly?", it didn't answer. Was the king deaf?

They swam nearer to it. It didn't move. Nervously, they touched it, and it didn't do anything. Soon the frogs had discovered that this was a king they could sit on, jump off, and call names, and they didn't think much of it. They called to Jove again.

"This king's useless!" they said. "We want a better one!"

Jove wasn't pleased. Who did these frogs think they were? He dropped an eel into the swamp. At least this one moved about.

The frogs watched their new king with great interest as it glided through the river, twisting and swishing. They called to it, swam after it, and offered it flies. But they soon discovered that their new king didn't pay any more attention than the log, and this time they were angry.

"This isn't funny!" the frogs called to Jove. "We want a proper king!"

This time, Jove was angry. He sent a heron, a thin, long-legged bird with a long sharp beak. The heron flew down, perched on a stone in the swamp, and looked down at the frogs with a small beady eye.

"That's better!" said the big green frog. "This king has noticed us!"

It certainly had. Herons are very fond of frogs. Before you could say, "Welcome, Your Majesty," it had swallowed two or three of them. It must have been a hungry heron, because in no time at all, it had gobbled down every single one.

LEAVE WELL ALONE!

The Milkmaid
and Her Pail

A FARMER'S DAUGHTER WAS walking through the rough forest paths to the market, carrying a pail of milk on her shoulder. Yes, on her shoulder, because that is what milkmaids used to do, and they did it very well. To while away the long walk, she began to think about how much money she would get for the milk and what she'd do with her share of it.

"It's good, creamy milk," she thought. "I can buy a few laying hens and a cockerel and sell the eggs, but not all of them. I'll let the hens hatch some and I'll rear them, so I'll have a whole flock of laying hens. The price of eggs is good just now, and if they're good layers I should be able to sell, say, a hundred a week. A year from now, I should have enough egg money for new summer clothes – a red dress would be nice."

She stepped carefully around
a puddle. "And if it's summer, I'll
need a hat," she thought out loud.
"A wide-brimmed one? Or a neat
little bonnet? And a shawl for when the
evenings are cool."

She had to stop for a moment, because
a stone had found its way into her old
wooden clogs. She shook it out, taking
care to keep the pail of milk steady, and
began to think about shoes.

"I'm sick to death of wearing clogs all
the time," she said. "When I have enough
egg money, I'll buy some soft, elegant
shoes to wear for best. And for dancing! I'd
love to have some dancing shoes! I'll go
to parties and dance beautifully, and
everyone will be so impressed! The
girls will be jealous, and the young
men…"

She was enjoying this idea so much
that she danced a few steps along

21

the path, holding her head high, forgetting to watch the uneven ground. A loose stone slipped away under her foot. Unable to help herself, she tripped and fell sprawling on the ground as the milk splashed away and sank uselessly into the earth.

The poor milkmaid sat in the middle of the path and cried. There was nothing to do now but go home, with no chickens and nothing to show for the day.

DON'T COUNT YOUR CHICKENS BEFORE THEY ARE HATCHED.

THE FOX AND THE CROW

THE CROW WASN'T much to look at. She was a big, heavy bird with a large black body too big for her small black head, beady little black eyes, and a beak that scared you just to look at it. That's not all. If you thought her looks were bad, you should have heard her voice. Or maybe you shouldn't.

"CRAA! CRAA!" It was all she ever sang, only she didn't sing at all. She croaked. Her voice might not have been tuneful, but, my word, it was loud. While the other birds twittered, whistled, chirped, and trilled, the crow squawked, "CRAA!" and frightened them all away.

The poor crow couldn't tell what was wrong with her voice. It was powerful, wasn't it? She thought it was really a very good voice, and she would fly across the forest singing while all the little animals ran away and hid.

One afternoon, she stopped making her horrible noise simply

because she had more important things to do with her beak. Some people had been having a picnic in the forest, and the crow gobbled down the leftover crusts and apple cores. A large piece of cheese had been dropped on the grass, so the crow picked it up and flew into a tree with it.

Not far away was the fox. Didn't I tell you how clever he was? The moment he saw that piece of cheese in the crow's mouth, he wanted it for himself.

It would be no good simply asking the crow to give him the cheese. The crow liked her food as much as she liked her singing voice. So the fox prowled below the tree, glanced up as if he'd hardly noticed her, and remarked, "Oh, dear! Cheese! That's not at all good for you. Not good at all."

The crow wasn't stupid. She knew what he wanted, and she kept that cheese firmly clamped in her beak. The fox tried again.

"How are you today?" he asked. Crow kept her mouth shut.

"Been busy?" he asked. The crow shrugged without opening her beak, so the fox tried a different approach.

"Your feathers look very nice today," he observed. Crow was supposed to open her beak and say "thank you". She didn't, but she gave a little flutter and looked pleased with herself. To Fox, this was a good sign.

"I've always thought your feathers were very beautiful," he went on. "They're so glossy, so long, so – er – so black. And you have such a charming little beak."

Crow looked down with pleasure at her own beak. Her eyes crossed, but she didn't drop the cheese.

"But what I admire most," said Fox, "is your voice." He saw the surprised look on the crow's face, and kept on talking. "The other animals and birds don't appreciate it. They're not real music lovers like you and me. It gives me such a thrill when I hear that lovely clear high note – you know the one I mean – that really stunning note that nobody else can reach…"

Crow couldn't resist any longer. "CRAAAA!" she shrieked. The other animals ran for cover, the cheese fell from her beak, and she was still cawing as Fox caught it and ran away to gobble it down and laugh.

NEVER TRUST A FLATTERER.

THE DOG IN THE MANGER

IN THE CORNER of the farmyard was a cowshed. In the corner of the cowshed was a manger.

A what?

A manger. It's a trough fastened to the wall, full of hay for animals to eat. A dog – a very bad-tempered dog – jumped into the manger, turned around four times, and settled himself down in the hay.

But dogs don't eat hay!

That's right, they don't. That's the point. The gentle brown and white cow was hungry, and came to the manger to eat. When she saw the dog, she asked it very politely to move so that she could eat the hay. But the dog only said, "Grrr! Grrrr! I'll bite!" He snapped at her and stayed put.

A donkey came to the manger and said, "Dinner time! Out you get, Dog!"

"Grrrrrrrr!" said the dog, baring his teeth. He snarled and snapped, so they both took a step backwards.

"Please?" said the donkey.

"Grrrow!" snarled the dog, and stayed put.

The tall, strong horse heard all this and decided to sort it out. She came into the cowshed.

"There's no need to be like that," she said. She was a very sensible animal. "There must be lots of places where you can lie down, all much more comfortable than our manger. But there's only one place where we can get our hay, so would you kindly lie down somewhere else? I'm sure we can find you some pleasant places."

The dog growled and snapped more than ever. "Go away! I'll bite!"

"This isn't doing anybody any good," said the horse. "Not even you, Dog." But the dog growled even more, said something very rude, and stayed put.

The cow, the donkey, and the horse looked at each other and realized that they might as well give up. They went outside to see if they could find a patch of grass.

"I don't understand," said the donkey. "Why won't he just get out of the manger?"

"Maybe he's just angry," said the cow.

"Maybe he's doing it just because he can," said the horse.

"Well, I still don't understand why he has to be so mean," said the donkey.

Do you?

IF YOU DON'T NEED IT, LET SOMEONE ELSE HAVE IT.

THE JAY AND THE
PEACOCKS

THERE WAS ONCE a jay. They really are nice-looking birds: about the size of magpies and pinkish-brown with blue on their wings, and what's the matter with that? But the jay in this story was not content to be a jay. He had seen peacocks strutting about with their long blue necks and their magnificent trailing tail feathers, and that was what he wanted. Everyone admired the peacocks, who could lift those tail feathers in the air like a fan and shake them. With their proud walk, their bright plumage, and that little coronet of feathers on their heads, they looked as if they ruled the earth. "I want to be a peacock," thought the jay.

This, of course, was impossible. A jay is a jay and a peacock is a peacock, and they're not alike. The jay should have realized this, but he was so keen to be a peacock that he wasn't thinking sensibly at all.

He used to watch the peacocks for hours at a time. He admired their beautiful feathers and their way of walking, lifting their feet delicately as if the ground wasn't fit for them to walk on. He'd copy that walk when nobody was looking. He was peering around a tree one day when, to his delight, he saw that a few peacock feathers lay on the ground. It must be moulting time for peacocks! By the time the peacocks went away in search of food, there was quite a little heap of feathers.

The jay hopped to the feathers and looked at them, sideways, as birds do. Then he darted forward to pick up the biggest feather with his beak, twisting round to poke it into his own tail. This wasn't easy, but after a lot of dropped and ruffled feathers he managed to fit a row of long peacock feathers into his wings and tail. He couldn't make his peacock tail stand up in a fan the way the real peacocks did, but he could trail it behind him without too many feathers falling out. He was very pleased with himself. He held up his head, practised the walk, and thought nobody could tell the difference between him and a genuine peacock.

When the real peacocks came back, shaking their tails, he strutted in among them, lifting his feet high and trailing his tail behind him, sure that they would welcome him as another splendid peacock, just as stately and magnificent as they were themselves.

"What's THAT?" screeched a peacock.

"I've no idea," squawked another. "Crow? Canary? Sparrow?

Whatever it is, it's dressed up in our feathers and pretending to be one of us. What a cheek!"

"Chase him!" cried the others, and they all ran after the poor jay, squawking and pulling at his borrowed feathers. As soon as he was safely out of the way, the jay hid and got his breath back.

If that was the way peacocks behaved, he decided, he wasn't going to stay with them. But he could still be a peacock! The real peacocks might have recognized that he wasn't one of their own kind, but the other jays probably didn't know much about peacocks. He picked up the feathers he had dropped and put them back on again. He could be a peacock among jays, and wouldn't they be impressed! When he saw a flock of jays, he strutted in among them.

"What's that?" asked a jay.

"It's a jay dressed up as a peacock," croaked another.

"Don't be silly!" said the jay. "I *am* a peacock. Don't you know what a peacock looks like?"

"Yes, we do," said the jays. "And they're nothing like you. You can show off with all the feathers you like. You're still a jay!"

FINE FEATHERS DON'T MAKE
FINE BIRDS.

THE FATHER AND HIS DAUGHTERS

FATHER SIMPLE WAS a contented man. Why wouldn't he be? True, his wife had died, and that was a great sorrow, but he had brought up his two daughters by himself and he loved them very dearly. His daughters were the great joy of his life, and he had done all he could for them, all their lives.

They were both grown up now and married, with homes of their own, but he visited them often and was always welcome to stay with them. They were kind-hearted, sensible girls, and loved their father. The elder daughter, Tabby, the tall, dark-haired one, had married a tilemaker and helped her husband to bake and paint the beautiful, decorated tiles people wanted for their paths and their walls. The younger daughter, little golden-haired Gwen, had married a gardener and worked hard in the gardens, helping him to grow vegetables, fruit, and flowers.

Early in the summer, Father Simple went to stay with his daughter Tabby. He admired her lovely house and the tilemaker's yard, where rows and rows of painted tiles lay in the sun to dry.

"Is there anything you need, my dear?" he asked her as they stood in the tileyard. "Is there any help I can give you – anything at all?"

Tabby smiled and shook her head. "We have everything we could possibly want," she said. "We have customers to buy the tiles, and as long as they go on buying them we'll always have business. We have our home, and we can afford the food and clothes we need. The only thing we want…" She bent down and touched a tile gently with her finger to see if the paint was dry.

"The only thing we want is a hot dry summer, so that the tiles will harden and the paint will dry in the heat."

After his stay with Tabby, Father Simple went to visit his younger daughter, Gwen. He admired her house, too, and the enormous garden, where she and her husband grew vegetables, delicious soft summer fruit, and tall colourful flowers.

"Is there anything you need, my dear?" asked Father Simple as they stood in the garden. "Is there anything at all that I can do to help you?"

"There's nothing that we need," said Gwen happily, taking his arm. "We have plenty of customers buying our produce at the market, and wealthy ladies and gentlemen come here to buy flowers. That all brings in plenty of money for all the things

we need. We're very happy. Except…"

"Yes?" asked Father Simple.

Gwen knelt down and crumbled some of the garden earth in her hand. She looked up at the sky.

"The gardens need rain," she said. "The only thing I still want is plenty of rain this summer, to keep the crops well watered and growing."

Father Simple took off his hat and scratched his head.

"One of my daughters needs sun, and the other needs rain!" he exclaimed. "So which of those am I to hope for?"

YOU CAN'T PLEASE EVERYONE.

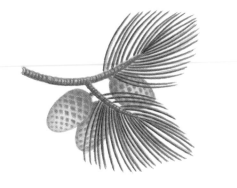

THE LIONESS

O N A SUMMER'S day, when the forest was just hot enough and shady enough for a pleasant afternoon out, the forest mothers took their children to play. Little monkeys swung through the branches, chattering at each other, puppies chased each other's tails, and a baby sloth hung asleep in a tree and fell off without waking up. Mother Fox arrived with her young, and Mother Hen gathered all her chickens together and hurried them away. The rabbit stayed near to her babies as Mother Goose marched over for a chat, with three gawky little goslings waddling along behind her.

"Aren't my babies doing well!" said Mother Goose. "All three of them, all thriving! How many young ones do you have now?"

"Eight," said the rabbit proudly, watching her little ones. "Eight, and all adorable. Aren't I lucky!"

Mother Dog felt a little jealous. "I had four in my last litter," she said. "I expect it will be more next time."

"Nine!" squeaked a mouse. "I may be small, but I had nine babies in my last litter!"

There was a sound of croaking behind them. Frogs were hopping in and out of a pool.

"Don't ask the frogs," said Mother Rabbit. "All that frogspawn and all those tadpoles. They lose count of their young."

"Tadpoles don't count," said Mother Goose firmly.

All this time, Lioness had been sitting up proudly, occasionally licking the fur of her handsome young lion cub, watching him as he stalked a butterfly. When she thought he might chase the puppies or run away into the forest, she would growl softly and place a firm paw on his tail. She heard all that the other animals were saying about the sizes of their families. Mother Fox approached her.

"Your Majesty," she said, "how many young ones do you have?"

Lioness called her cub to her. Young as he was, he moved with grace and strength, carrying his head high and happy.

"I have only one," said Lioness. "But that one is a lion!"

QUALITY IS MORE IMPORTANT
THAN QUANTITY.

BELLING THE CAT

"BE VERY, VERY quiet."

The youngest mouse *was* trying very hard to be quiet. It was the middle of the night and long after her bedtime, but she was holding her mother's paw as they scurried along under the floorboards of the big house. This evening, there was to be an Important Meeting of the Mouse Safety Committee and the youngest mouse wasn't supposed to be there at all, but her mother and father were both members of the Mouse Safety Committee and couldn't find a babysitter, so the youngest mouse had to go with them.

"Be very, very quiet!" Mother had told her, so that was what the youngest mouse was doing, though she had to bite her tongue in the effort to stay silent. There was a swish as her tail whisked round a corner.

"Shh!" said Mother, frowning down at her. The youngest

mouse picked up her tail and carried it in her mouth to stop it from dragging, and pattered along to the meeting.

The Mouse Hall was in a space in the wall behind a fireplace, which made it warm. It was lit with leftover bits of candles, and the head mouse – or the Wisest Whiskers, as he was called – stood behind a pebble that he used as a desk. The youngest mouse, who had never been to anything like this before, was about to say how exciting it was and dropped her tail, but then she remembered to be very, very quiet and stopped, and put her tail in her mouth again to make sure she didn't interrupt by accident. The grown-ups weren't being quiet at all. They were chattering all around her, but they stopped as soon as the Wisest Whiskers rang a bell (it had dropped off a Christmas decoration many years ago) as a signal to be quiet.

The mice settled down to listen. The Wisest Whiskers stood up, said a lot of things about welcoming them all to the meeting, and started his speech.

"Field Mice and House Mice," he began, "we have called this meeting because all our mouse colonies are in the greatest danger. The people who live in this house have – I am sorry to tell you – bought a CAT!"

The youngest mouse was so shocked that she jumped, bit her tail by accident, and squeaked, but nobody noticed. All the other mice were squeaking and shaking, and the Wisest Whiskers had to ring the bell again to calm them all down. Mother took the youngest mouse's paw.

"We must do something about this terrible situation," said the Wisest Whiskers. "No mouse can gather crumbs in safety

while a cat prowls the house. If a cat could be more like a dog, there would be no problem. We can hear a dog wherever it is in the house. Cats are quiet, secretive animals that creep up on a mouse and spring to kill. The garden is no safer – the cat has been seen sniffing silently along the flowerbeds. We must take action. What are we going to do about this cat? Has anyone any suggestions?"

One mouse put up his paw and suggested that they frighten the cat away, but nobody could think of anything mice could do to scare a cat. Another suggested dropping a net on top of the cat and trapping it, but the Wisest Whiskers said that the cat would only escape, or yowl until the people came to let it out. Someone said that they could leave poisoned fish in the garden for it, but another pointed out that they didn't know where they could get any fish, and somebody else said that they didn't know where to get any poison either, so that idea was dropped. Soon everyone was putting up their paws and having bright ideas, and the Wisest Whiskers rang his bell again.

A grown-up mouse held up his paw. "Sir," he said, "everybody notices when you ring your bell. So if we put a bell on the cat, we would all be able to hear her coming."

The youngest mouse frowned, because she could see something wrong with this idea, but nobody else seemed to think there was a problem. Everybody was saying that it was the perfect solution and offering to find a bell and make a collar. Very shyly, the youngest mouse raised her paw.

"Shh!" whispered Mother. "I've told you to be very, very quiet!"

The Wisest Whiskers only smiled quietly. "That's all right," he said. "Let's hear what the youngest mouse wants to say. What have you to tell us, young mouse?"

"Please, sir," said the youngest mouse, "we need to get the collar onto the cat. We need a mouse who'll go right up to her and put it round her neck."

"Exactly," said the Wisest Whiskers. "Do we have a volunteer?"

Then everyone was very, very quiet.

GREAT IDEAS ARE EASIER
SAID THAN DONE.

THE LARK AND HER YOUNG

SPRINGTIME CAME, AND the first crops began to push their way
through the earth. The meadow became green with young
wheat that rippled in the breeze. Soon it was high enough for
the lark to build her nest there and lay her eggs, all hidden deep
among the growing crop. From three warm eggs hatched three
tiny chicks, hungry, scrawny little scraps with gaping beaks and
comical faces. They didn't stay like that for long. Soon they had
feathers and were learning to hop about using their wings.

Day by day, as spring turned to summer, the three chicks grew
bigger and stronger. So did the wheat in the field. The days
lengthened, and the sunshine ripened the crop.

The first chick to hatch was the quickest to learn, and before
long he could fly above the wheat. When the farmer came out
to take a look at the crop, the young lark was watching and
listening.

The farmer took a few ears of wheat, rubbed them in his fingers, and bit them. "This wheat is ready to cut," he said. "I'll call on my friends and neighbours and ask them to come and help me with harvesting it."

The young lark was alarmed. What would happen to them and their nest if the farmer and his friends came with their sharp scythes, cutting down the wheat? He flew back to his mother.

"Mother, we must go!" he warned her. "The farmer says he's going to call on his neighbours and ask them to come and help him cut down the wheat! We have to escape — now!" But Mother Lark only smiled calmly.

"There's no need to do anything yet, my dear," she said. "He's only sending a message around a few friends. He doesn't mean it."

The young lark forgot about it, and went on learning to fly and to feed himself. A week later, he was flying up above the wheat again when he heard the farmer coming. He hid, watched, and listened as the farmer rubbed wheat between his finger and thumb, and bit it.

"This shouldn't wait any longer," said the farmer. "I'll do it myself! I'll bring my sons and all my own workers down here tomorrow, and we'll get all this lot in."

The young lark flew back to his mother and told her what the farmer had said.

"Did he say exactly that?" she asked. "His sons and all his workers are coming to help him tomorrow?"

"Yes, Mother," said the young lark.

"Then, children, you must be ready to fly!" said the mother lark. "All that talk about his neighbours was never going to come to anything. But if he's made up his mind to do the work himself tomorrow, he really means it, and tomorrow this field will be cut to the ground. Little ones, we must leave!"

SELF-HELP IS THE
BEST HELP.

THE MISER AND HIS GOLD

Do you know what a miser is? If you think it sounds a bit like "miserable", you're right. It is. And Titus Pennypinch was as mean as any miser could be.

Misers keep all their money in a safe place and never, ever spend any of it if they can help it. A miser might have whole rooms full of money, but he'd live on porridge and bean soup to save money on food. A miser would wear his old clothes until there were huge raggy holes in the elbows of his sweaters.

On winter days, when icicles clung to the walls of her house, a miser would put on three sets of underwear, two sweaters, two pairs of thick leggings, her shabby old winter coat, scarf, hat, and mittens so she wouldn't have to spend money on coal or wood for the fire. As for buying anyone a present, a miser wouldn't dream of it! The very thought of buying presents would give a miser indigestion (or maybe that would be the bean soup).

Titus Pennypinch had enough gold to live very comfortably for the rest of his life and still give money away. He could have paid for all his own needs, hot dinners for all the old people in his village, winter coats for all the children, and a party every year, and still have money to spare. Instead, he lived like a poor man in a cold, tumbledown house, wearing shabby old clothes and eating boiled cabbage now and again as a change from the porridge and bean soup.

The cabbage was one of his treats. He only allowed himself two treats. The other one – his big treat – was to go down to a particular tree in his garden and dig. Beside this tree he had buried his gold. He would dig until he found his box of gold pieces, then he would take them all out, sort them out into neat little heaps, and count them. Then he would give a greedy, gloating giggle and bury it all again.

When Titus was looking at his gold, he was so absorbed that he didn't notice anything else at all. Maybe that's why he never thought of looking around to see if anyone was watching. One day, somebody was.

A thief was hanging around the village, keeping out of sight, looking out for anything worth stealing. When he saw the miser examining his gold and burying it again, he couldn't believe his luck. He waited until dark, when Titus was asleep, stole the gold, and filled in the hole again.

Three days later, terrible wailing and moaning came from Titus's house, so loud that everyone in the village heard it and thought someone was being murdered. They all ran toward the sound and found Titus on his knees by a hole in the ground,

weeping, howling, and banging his fists on the ground.

"It's gone!" he moaned. "My beautiful gold! Every single penny of it! Every last one! It's been stolen, all my gold!"

One of his neighbours, a newcomer to the village, looked into the empty hole and then at Titus. He didn't look like a rich man.

"What did you do with your gold?" he asked.

"I didn't do anything with it!" snapped Titus. "I just kept it here and looked at it!"

"You never spent any of it?" asked the newcomer.

"No!" cried Titus. "Not a penny. I only came here to look at it!"

"Well, in that case," said the newcomer, "the gold hasn't made any difference to your life or anybody else's. You might as well come here and look at the hole in the ground. It'll do you just as much good."

IF GOOD THINGS AREN'T USED,
THEY MIGHT AS WELL NOT
EXIST.

THE FOX AND THE CRANE

T HE FOX WAS the most cunning animal in the forest – or so everyone thought.

The fox invited the crane to supper. Some birds would have flown right out of the forest rather than go to supper with the fox, but the crane, who was a tall, thin bird with a long sharp beak like a pair of tongs, accepted. She polished her beak and smoothed her feathers and arrived outside the fox's lair, where a tablecloth had been spread over a tree stump. The fox, with the foxiest of smiles, strolled out to meet her.

"How very sweet of you to come and keep a poor lonely fox company," he said. "For such a simple supper, too. And it is, my dear, a very simple supper. I hope soup will be enough."

The fox went back to his lair and returned, carrying two shallow dishes of soup, which he put on the table. Now, the crane didn't mind at all that there was only soup for supper.

What she did find difficult the dish the fox placed before her. It was very easy for the fox, who lapped it up the way a dog laps water, but the poor crane could only stab and poke at it with her long beak, and hardly managed to swallow anything at all. She pecked, she struggled, she spilt soup on the tablecloth, and the worst thing of all was the way she could feel the fox looking at her. He had finished lapping up his soup and was watching her, cleaning his whiskers and enjoying her embarrassment with a sly smile on his face.

Did the crane snap at him with her long sharp beak? No. She thanked him very politely, even though she'd hardly eaten a thing.

"Now, Fox," she said, "I've had such a lovely evening, I would be delighted if you'd come to supper with me one day. Shall we say in a week's time?"

The fox was surprised, but he was still pleased with himself and was hoping for more fun. He told the crane he would love to come and that he was looking forward to it, which was true.

A week later, the fox arrived to have supper with the crane. She, too, had spread a tablecloth over a tree stump, and again she had polished her beak and smoothed her feathers.

"My dear Fox," she said, "how kind of you to come and keep a lonely crane company. It's only soup, but I know you like that. I'm afraid I only have a pitcher to serve it in, so we'll have to take turns. Guests first, of course."

"Better and better!" thought the fox, who neither knew nor cared what a pitcher was. He was already planning to finish all the soup before the crane's turn. He sat down at the table and, from behind it, the crane picked up what she called the pitcher. It was a very tall thin jug with a narrow neck. The crane smiled sweetly as she placed it on the table.

"Do help yourself," she said.

The fox stared at the pitcher. He prowled around it, trying to work out a way of reaching it, then stood on the table on his hind paws, but he still couldn't reach the top of the pitcher. He tried to tip it toward himself, but it was too tall and heavy for him to handle.

Finally, the crane said, "Poor Fox! Can't you manage? Here, let me show you what to do."

She plunged her long beak into the narrow neck of the pitcher and drank all she wanted.

Then she straightened up, wiped her beak neatly on the grass, and said, "Now, Fox – would you like to try again?"

TREAT OTHERS AS YOU WANT
THEM TO TREAT YOU.

THE DONKEY AND HER SHADOW

IMAGINE A DAY so hot and sunny that you can feel your skin turning red and your shirt sticking to you. Now imagine you are walking along a dry, dusty road in a bare, rocky landscape with no trees, no shadow. This is what's happening in this story of three travellers walking that hot, hard road.

The first traveller was a merchant, a tall man with a hard face, taking bundles of cloth to sell at market. By a length of long rope he led the second traveller, who was a shaggy grey donkey. She was the one who carried all those bales of cloth, slung on baskets called panniers on either side of her. The third traveller had the muscles of a builder and a head like a boulder, and he was the donkey's owner. He stayed very close to her. That's not because he was fond of her. If he'd been fond of her, he wouldn't have hired her out to the merchant to load her up with all those heavy bales on such a day.

You may wonder why, if he'd hired the donkey to the merchant, the owner went with them. That's because he didn't trust the merchant to bring her back. Besides, somebody else at the market might hire her to carry goods home. So both the merchant and the owner expected to make good money that day. The donkey didn't expect anything much. She was hoping for a drink, a rest, and something to eat, but who cared about her? The men were hot, grumpy, and suspicious of each other, so they trudged along without speaking. (By now you've probably worked out that the donkey was the only one worth speaking *to*, and she was too tired even to bray.)

They came at last to a little spring of fresh water, and the donkey's ears twitched hopefully.

"Good place to stop for a drink," grunted the owner to the merchant. "And while we're having a break, take those panniers off my donkey. She'll be no use to me if she collapses in the heat."

"It wouldn't do me and my cloth any good, either," muttered the merchant as he lifted the load from her back and tied the end of the rope to a tree. The donkey gave herself a little shake and, as the rope left her plenty of room to move, took a good drink from the spring. The men drank and splashed water on their faces and sat down to rest. The merchant sat in the coolness of the donkey's shadow.

"Excuse me!" growled the owner. "That shadow belongs to me!" He tried to get into the shade, too, but there was only

room for one. She was just a little donkey.

"But it's only a shadow!" exclaimed the merchant. "Its shadow doesn't belong to anyone!"

"Oh, but it does," argued the owner. "The shadow goes with the donkey, and the donkey's my property. You only paid to hire the donkey, not the shadow. Shadows are extra."

"Ridiculous!" said the merchant. "You can't demand money for a shadow!"

"I can and I will!" said the owner. "And if you won't pay, you can get out of there!" He tried to push the merchant out of the shadow, and the merchant pushed back.

All this time, the donkey had enjoyed a good long drink and a mouthful or two of rough grass and felt a lot better. She felt so much better that while the merchant and the owner were quarrelling, she decided to see what the rope tasted like. It was a bit like thistles, and she chewed patiently at it.

"That donkey is mine!" roared the owner, pushing the merchant.

"I paid for her, shadow and all!" shouted the merchant, barging at the owner.

"Chisel-face!" yelled the owner as he swung a punch at the merchant.

"Boulder-head!" called the merchant, swinging a bale of cloth at the owner.

All this time, the donkey had been chewing on the rope, and at last she had chewed right through it. The two men were still fighting and paying no attention to her, so she trotted off to where the grass looked nicer. She felt ready for a gallop after that.

At last, the merchant and the owner, tired, hot, and sweaty, picked themselves up and staggered to the spring to wash their hands and faces.

"Where's the donkey?" demanded the owner. But the donkey was miles away, where there were trees, streams, and delicious grass, and they would never find her.

If you try to keep the shadow, you lose the real thing.

THE SILKWORM AND THE SPIDER

THE LITTLE SILKWORM was very excited. She had been asked to make twenty yards of silk for the lion princess's wedding veil, and she set to work to do her very best spinning. She began to work a fine thread, smooth and gleaming. As she worked, a spider came in and watched for a little while.

"Miss Silkworm, is there room for two of us in here?" she asked. "I need to spin a web."

"Help yourself," said the silkworm without stopping her work. "There's plenty of room."

So the spider climbed into a high corner by the window and began to weave her web. For a while, there was no sound in the workroom at all apart from the spider whispering to herself now and again, "Over, under, over, under…"

The spider worked quickly, with all eight legs spinning and weaving, and soon her web was complete. She swung from a thread to look at it and admire it.

"Though I say it myself, that is a very nice piece of work," she remarked. "Miss Silkworm, would you like to see?"

The silkworm had established a steady rhythm in her spinning and didn't like being interrupted. However, she always tried to be polite, so she stopped to look up at the web.

"It's very neat," she observed. "I do like that design." Then she went on spinning her silk.

The spider was offended. Her webs were very fine and she felt the silkworm should have been more impressed. What could a silkworm do, anyway? Make silk, that's all. She couldn't weave a web. She ought to show respect to a superior craftswoman.

"So what are you doing, Miss Silkworm?" she asked, swinging from a corner of her web. "Do let me see. Oh, just plain silk. Plain and simple. But that's all you do, isn't it? No pattern. I suppose that's all you can manage."

"Yes, that's what I do," said the silkworm calmly. "Plain and simple silk, but it is the best silk. Your webs may be very intricate, and you make them beautifully, but what are they for? They're only fly traps, and in a day or two they become dirty, flimsy cobwebs, and people sweep them away. They have special brushes for brushing away cobwebs, don't they? But my plain and simple silk will be worn by royalty, and everybody will see it. It will be kept and admired for years to come."

THE FINEST ART WILL LAST.

THE CLOWN AND THE
COUNTRYMAN

EVERY MARKET DAY, a stage was set up in the town square. The square was always full of people on those days, buying, selling, gossiping, and wanting to be entertained. That might have meant throwing rotten cabbages at the poor entertainers if they weren't very good, but that didn't stop singers, dancers, acrobats, clowns, jugglers, and people who did animal impressions from having a go.

You could sing for the crowds, if you thought your voice was good enough. If it wasn't, you'd soon find out. You could dance, but the platform was a bit rickety. There were some very unusual acts – fire-eaters, a bagpipe player, and the man who danced a hornpipe with a ferret on his head – but the crowd's favourite was Grimbo the Clown.

On this particular market day in spring, Grimbo had a new trick, which was to imitate the sound of a piglet squealing. The crowd gathered around and laughed helplessly as Grimbo squeaked, grunted, and pulled faces, but one man who didn't laugh was the countryman.

The countryman was a farmer who had come to market to sell the pigs he had reared. As a man who worked with pigs every day, he was very familiar with the noises they made and didn't think much of Grimbo's impression. When the clown came down from the stage, the countryman climbed up.

"Ladies and gentlemen," he called, "I may not be a clown, but I know all about pigs. Mr Grimbo, I challenge you to a squeal-like-a-piglet contest next market day."

"Done!" said Grimbo. The next market day, everyone gathered

round the stage to hear the Battle of the Squeal.

Grimbo appeared first and did his piglet imitation, which by now was famous. The crowd laughed, cheered, applauded, and waited gleefully to see how the countryman compared.

The countryman appeared and did his piglet impression without any of Grimbo's face-pulling. The crowd wasn't impressed.

"I think nothing of that," muttered one man.

"Go home!" shouted another, and the countryman ducked as a cabbage flew past him and hit the hornpipe dancer, who was waiting to come on. Unanimously, the crowd proclaimed Grimbo the winner.

"In that case," said the countryman, "I can see you know nothing about pigs!" And from behind his back he produced a small, pink, squealing piglet.

(You may like to know that the hornpipe dancer and his ferret were unhurt and the piglet ate the cabbage.)

PEOPLE OFTEN PREFER THE IMITATION
TO THE REAL THING.

ANDROCLES AND THE LION

I N THE FOREST the trees cast long evening shadows, and the creatures of the night were waking. The man lost in the forest couldn't see them, but he could hear the noise as they barked, bayed, and growled. It was frightening, but it was better than being a slave.

Androcles had been owned by a cruel master, and his life had been one of hunger, heavy work, and beatings, day after day, until he had run away. If he were caught, he would be killed, so he had to stay hidden in the forest and find a way to survive there. He wasn't sure what he would eat, but there must be berries and wild plants, he thought, and he could trap animals for meat. He'd find a cave to sleep in and he knew how to light fires, not just to keep himself warm, but to scare away dangerous beasts. His life would not be easy, but it would be better than slavery.

He didn't fear hunger or cold. There were only two things

that scared him. He feared the wild animals that prowled in the forest. He feared their size, their great power and strength, their sharp teeth and red mouths, and their long tearing claws. Secondly, he was afraid of being caught. Runaway slaves were always put to death.

He found a spring of fresh water and a cave, where he lit a fire at the entrance and huddled beside it, hardly sleeping at all. At morning light he went out into the forest, looking for food and keeping a wary eye out for savage beasts. Being a slave, he owned no weapons, so he carried a sharpened stick to protect himself and held it firmly in both hands as he wove his way between the trees, listening for any sound of danger.

Among the birdsong and the rustle of wind in the branches, he heard a low, steady growl. Androcles gripped his stick tightly in both hands and crept toward the sound.

Under the shadow of a tree lay a lion, his mane shaggy and his fur bloodied. He growled at Androcles, showing his teeth. Androcles stood in the shadow of the trees, watching, and soon he no longer noticed the lion's strength, nor his teeth and claws. What he noticed was the pain in the poor beast's half-closed eyes, and the injured and bloodstained paw the lion held up. A sharp thorn was embedded in the pad.

Androcles hesitated. He shouldn't go near that lion. Wounded or not, it would savage him as soon as he went near it, and an injured animal is always a frightened animal, ready to defend itself. If he tried to help it, it might take his hand off. But he saw how it suffered and that it would die if it stayed there without help, so he knelt down in front of it.

"Gently now, lion," he said, and stroked it to calm it. "I won't hurt you. Shh. Lie still."

As gently he could, he drew out the thorn. The wound was deep and could become infected, so he brought water from the spring to wash it and moss to stop the bleeding.

"And now," he thought, taking a step backward as the lion raised its head, "now it's feeling better, it's sure to eat me."

The lion licked Androcles' hand. When Androcles went to look for something to eat, the lion padded along beside him, limping a little, doing him no harm. It walked back to the cave with him, and that night they lay down by the same fire.

In the morning, when Androcles was very hungry, the lion came to the mouth of the cave with a freshly killed rabbit, which he dropped on the floor for Androcles to eat. When Androcles went out into the forest, the lion went with him to keep dangerous beasts away, and they shared the cave and the fire at night.

They might have lived like this for years, but it seemed that Androcles wouldn't be so lucky. Soldiers came to the forest. Androcles was arrested as a runaway slave and taken to the city in chains to be put to death.

At that time, runaway slaves met a particularly cruel death. They were taken to the amphitheatre so that everybody could get a good view, and wild animals would be sent in so that everyone could watch the poor slaves being torn apart and eaten by the beasts. The animals were deliberately kept hungry – so hungry that they'd jump straight at their poor victims and take them apart.

After a hungry night in a cold, damp dungeon, Androcles was

led out by guards to the arena. The sudden sunlight dazzled him, and the noise hit his ears – shouting, cheering, booing, and chanting rose from the crowd. He turned slowly around to look at them, wondering what was so exciting about his miserable death, then gazed up at the blue sky above him and hoped it would all soon be over.

With a clank and a rattle, a door was opened. The crowd shrieked and gasped as a lion padded steadily toward the lonely figure in the centre of the ring. The lion roared. Then Androcles' face lit up with the brightest smile anyone had ever seen. He fell to his knees, laughing, and stretched out his arms. It was *his* lion! The lion trotted up to him, licked his face, and lay down, settling his head on Androcles' lap.

There was a moment of astonished silence from the crowd, then they all began whispering as Androcles and the lion greeted one another. One of the guards approached to separate them, but the lion snarled at him, and he retreated quickly as the crowd – which was on Androcles' side by now – clapped and cheered.

Androcles stood up, rubbed his face because his eyes were watering, and rested his hand on the lion's mane. In the high gold royal box, the emperor was beckoning him.

Still in his dirty old tunic, Androcles stood before the emperor and told his story. The emperor was so impressed that he pardoned Androcles at once and made him a free man, so that he could live in the city in safety. The lion was freed, too, and released to return to the forest he loved. But now that Androcles could go wherever he liked, he often made his way back to the forest, to meet his old friend again.

GRATITUDE IS A SIGN OF A NOBLE NATURE.

THE MONKEY AND THE DOLPHIN

THIS IS THE story of the monkey and the dolphin, but it begins as the story of the monkey and the sailor.

The sailor was going on a long voyage and wanted something to keep him amused. The rest of the sailors weren't very amusing company, unless you thought all that shouting of "aye-aye sir", "run up the yardarm, me hearties", and "shiver me what-d'you-call-it" was funny, so the sailor bought a monkey. The monkey kept everyone very amused by pulling their hats off, untying all the knots, dropping fruit skins, blowing whistles loudly in the middle of the night, and lying around where you'd trip over him.

Some people said that it was the monkey's fault that the ship sank, but it wasn't. He was asleep in the cat basket as they sailed toward the coast of Greece when a sudden violent tempest broke

out, tossing the ship from side to side and throwing wild waves over the deck. Shouting orders to each other, the sailors all ran onto the deck and fought with all their strength to save the ship. Oh, but she couldn't be saved. As she sank helplessly to the bottom of the sea, men and monkey leaped into the water and swam for their lives.

Swimming nearby and not at all alarmed by the storm was a dolphin, and dolphins are friendly to humans. Seeing a small figure struggling to stay afloat and thinking, in the darkness and the wild waves, that it was human, the dolphin swam to his rescue.

"I'm here!" cried the dolphin. Strong and graceful, he swam underneath the monkey, lifting it onto his back and carrying it away. "I'll take you to the shore! Hold on!"

As the dolphin carried the monkey safely away, the tempest calmed and the sun lightened the sky. At last, the famous city of Athens came into sight.

"There it is!" said the dolphin. "There's Athens! There isn't a city like it anywhere in the world! Do you come from Athens?"

"Oh, yes!" said the monkey. He didn't, but he thought the dolphin would be impressed by having an Athenian passenger. "Oh, I'm glad to see it again! My family have lived in Athens for generations. We're one of the oldest Athenian families. Everybody knows us."

"Then your family must be well respected in the city," remarked the dolphin.

"Respected?" said the monkey. "Whenever there are important decisions to be made, they ask us. Oh, and by the way, my grandfather was a duke. I don't think I mentioned that."

"Is that so?" said the dolphin. The more his passenger talked, the less he sounded like an Athenian. "Do you know Piraeus?"

This was a trick question, to find out how much the passenger really knew. Piraeus was the harbour city in Athens.

"Piraeus!" exclaimed the monkey. "Do I know him? I knew him before he was famous! We were at school together! Last time I saw him…"

The monkey never finished the sentence. The dolphin now knew that the passenger was lying and wasn't going to carry a liar any further. With a flip and a splash he threw the monkey into the sea and swam away, leaving him to look after himself.

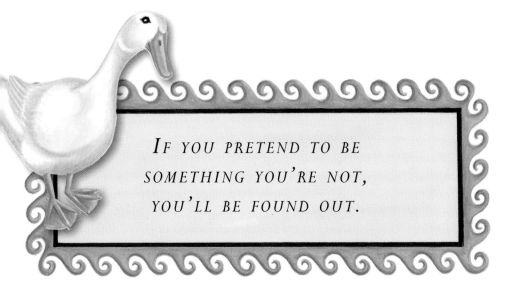

IF YOU PRETEND TO BE SOMETHING YOU'RE NOT, YOU'LL BE FOUND OUT.

THE SWALLOW AND THE
OTHER BIRDS

THE SWALLOW IS a wise bird. She flies high, and as she flies, she is hunting. She swoops down on the insects in the air, feeding as she soars through the wide blue sky. She stays far out of the reach of cats and foxes, and she never stays to starve through the freezing winters. She flies south to the heart of Africa and only returns in spring. She knows about surviving in a world full of danger.

One day, as she swooped and soared, snapping up the flies, Madam Swallow caught sight of something that made her curious. Far below, she could see the ridge and furrows of the land and a farmer sowing seeds in a field. The small birds pecked about for their food, looking very tiny from such a great height.

The swallow flew down to perch on a fence post. She folded

her wings to watch, and when she saw what the farmer was sowing, she spread out her wings and cried out a warning.

"Birds! Birds!" she sang. "The farmer is sowing hemp seed, hemp seed! You must pick it up, every single seed! You mustn't let it grow, or it will destroy you!"

The birds took no notice. They were enjoying their feast of worms and small beetles, and there were tastier seeds than hemp to feed on.

"Listen to me!" she sang. "You must pick up every speck of the hemp. If it grows, it will kill you!"

The birds looked at each other. "What does she know about seeds? She eats insects! Take no notice of her!"

The swallow herself cleared away all the hemp she could and carried the seeds away to where they could do no harm. But most of them stayed in the field, where they grew and grew.

When the hemp was fully grown, it was tall, thick, and strong. When it was cut, the farmer had it made into rope. He needed thin, strong rope.

What does a farmer need rope for? For tethering animals. For tying bales of hay to carts. And for making nets to spread across his fields and trap the small birds as soon as they come to peck at his crops. The birds who hadn't listened to Madam Swallow were caught and trapped in those nets, and though they flapped and struggled with all their might, they could not escape. The swallow was distressed, but she could do nothing to help them.

"Birds, birds, why didn't you listen to me?" she cried. "I told you the hemp would destroy you! If only you had stopped it when you had the chance!"

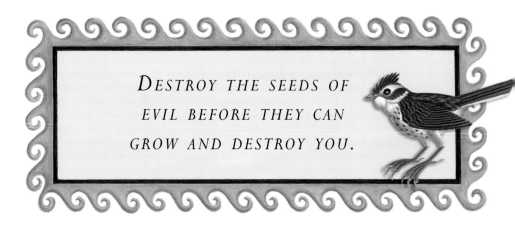

DESTROY THE SEEDS OF
EVIL BEFORE THEY CAN
GROW AND DESTROY YOU.

THE NORTH WIND
AND THE SUN

THE NORTH WIND is a bully. His breath is as bitter as the winter nights and as powerful as rage. It has cruel fingers that claw and sting with cold.

The sun just shines. That's all he does.

A traveller was on his way down a long, winding road on a spring morning. There was a light breeze and a touch of early morning coolness in the air, so he wore his cloak (his old green one) and his hat (the brown one that his mother made). The north wind looked down at him with an unpleasant smile.

"I could tear that cloak from his back from here," he said.

The sun glanced down. "That would not be difficult," he said.

"Not difficult!" snapped the north wind. "Not difficult! You wouldn't be able to do it!"

"Wouldn't I?" asked the sun mildly.

"Then I'll challenge you," said the north wind, who was getting angry. "We'll each see if we can get that cloak off him."

"You'll go first, I suppose?" said the sun.

For an answer, the north wind filled his great lungs with air that chilled as he inhaled it. With his first breath, he blew a grey cloud in front of the sun. Then he breathed a chill wind at the traveller, who only frowned up at the sky and wrapped his cloak around himself.

The north wind didn't mind about this because he hadn't even started. He blew harder, making fierce, powerful gusts so that leaves on the trees shuddered, fell, and danced along the road. The traveller held on to his hat with one hand and his old green cloak with the other, gripping more tightly with every blast.

The north wind blew harder, bending the trees. Plant pots tipped over and smashed, gates rattled, animals ran for shelter, washing was torn from the lines, and the traveller clutched his cloak more firmly than ever.

The north wind raged and roared. He gathered up icy Siberian gales, Arctic storms, and hurricanes, and flung them with all his might at the traveller. Slates blew from the rooftops and smashed on the ground, and the traveller struggled. His head was down, his shoulders were up, and his frozen hands still clutched at his cloak and his hat. When he couldn't walk another step, he

sheltered under a tree with his back to the wind, shivering and gripping his cloak and hat with fingers so cold they were numb until, at last, the wind dropped. The north wind was exhausted.

The sun looked out from behind the cloud. "Have you finished?" he asked mildly. "Then it's my turn now."

The north wind had no breath left to answer him. So the sun rose high above the clouds, smiling. He shone on the road, on the tree, and on the traveller.

The traveller, huddled under the tree, stepped out. "This is better," he thought. "There's real warmth in that sun." He straightened up and went on his way as the sun shone. Now that the wind had dropped, he no longer clung to his cloak and hat. As the sunshine grew stronger, he sang as he walked, until he needed to stop and have a drink. First, he took off his hat (the brown one his mother made) and fanned himself with it. Then, with a contented smile, he took off his old green cloak, spread it on the ground, sat down, and took a long, long drink from his water bottle.

And the sun just shone.

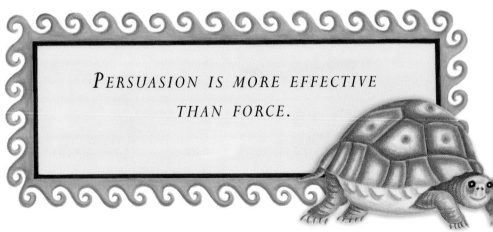

PERSUASION IS MORE EFFECTIVE
THAN FORCE.

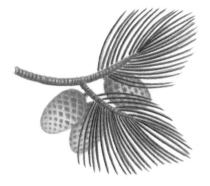

THE FOX AND THE
LEOPARD

THE FOX HAD a coat of deep red-brown, the colour of leaves in autumn. His nose was long, his ears were pointed, and his eyes were as dark and as glinting as berries in the dew and missed nothing. His thick brush of a tail was almost as long as his body. He was a splendid fox and as clever as any creature could be. He was fast on his paws, too, and quick and cunning enough to get himself out of trouble.

If the fox was in danger, his head stayed cool and his mind sharp. Even when he stepped into a clearing and found the long, lean leopard basking in a patch of sunlight, the fox didn't panic. The leopard was a fast animal with a taste for fresh meat, but everyone knew that fox meat tasted unpleasant and caused indigestion. (The fox, by the way, had made sure that everyone knew that.)

The leopard was a refined animal and particular about his food, and would never eat anything so coarse and gristly as fox. As the fox approached, the leopard lazily raised his head.

"Nice coat," remarked the leopard. "What a pity that it's all one colour. Don't you ever wish you had spots like me?"

The fox liked his deep red-brown coat exactly the way it was, but there was no point in saying so. The leopard liked to talk about himself and especially about his spotted coat.

"The useful thing about spots is that they're perfect for camouflage," he said. "If I hadn't looked up when you arrived, you wouldn't have seen me at all."

"That must be a sad thing for an animal who lies around waiting to be looked at," thought the fox, but he knew better than to say so.

"Yes, I see," he said. "They're perfect for camouflage in dappled shade or on stony ground, but if…"

"Where else would I want to be?" drawled the leopard. "And, you know, I'm so glad to be a leopard. Lions are supposed to be golden brown, but they're more of a pale mud colour. Tigers have stripes," he flicked his tail with irritation, "and I get a headache just looking at those hideous stripes, don't you?"

"I keep clear of tigers," thought the fox, but he knew that the leopard wouldn't want to hear that.

"The important thing is to vary the spots," pursued the leopard. "Do you see? These aren't just any old spots! The ones on my flank look like paw prints! This one here, just by my hip, that's my favourite. It's very unusual. And I do love being glossy. What's it like having a rough coat like yours?"

"It keeps me warm in winter and cool in the summer," said the fox, growing tired of letting the leopard have it all his own way. "I'm very happy with it."

"But it's not a thing of beauty," purred the leopard. "Everywhere I go, I carry these beautiful spots with me, and every single one is a little piece of perfection."

"Enough is enough," thought the fox. He surveyed the leopard's skin.

"Yes, I admit it," he said at last. "Such perfect spots and so beautifully arranged. But, Leopard, I can escape from the hunter with his dogs and fast horses. I can find food in the harshest winter and steal hens from under the farmer's nose. So, you have a beautifully decorated coat, but I have what you might call a highly decorated mind. I think that's so much more important."

The leopard sat up to argue. But the fox had vanished into the trees, and there was no more trace of him.

BEAUTY IS ONLY SKIN-DEEP.

THE ANT AND THE
GRASSHOPPER

ALL SUMMER, THROUGH the hot and dusty days, the ants worked hard. When the birds rose up and sang to the dawn, they could see the ants, thousands of them, marching through the forest, carrying twigs and pieces of leaf to their anthill. In the heat of the day, when the animals were glad to lie down in the cool shade of the trees to rest and the earth was hot underfoot, the ants worked on, marching, carrying, storing, and building as they built up their anthill and filled it with food. When the sun sank, the bats flew, and the hedgehogs crept out for supper, even then, a few strong, determined ants would be busy.

"Make all ready! Make all ready!" they chanted as they marched. "Food for the queen! Food for the queen!" they repeated as they piled up the leaves. Some of those leaves were so big that it took eight strong ants to carry them, but the queen must be fed, the house must be strong, and the stores must be full.

A bright green grasshopper was singing as the ants marched past. He had been singing all day, but when he saw the columns of busy ants working in the midday sun, he couldn't sing for laughing.

An ant stopped and glared up at him. "What's so funny?" it demanded.

"You... you are!" gasped the grasshopper. "What are you doing that for?"

"We're getting ready for the winter," said the ant, and the grasshopper laughed so much he rolled over helplessly on to his back and kicked his legs in the air. The ants marched on past. They had seen some crumbs dropped by a traveller, and these had to be picked up and carried back to the colony.

"Ready for the winter! Ready for the winter!" chanted the ants. They piled up their stores in the anthill and marched out for more, never keeping still, foraging for winter stores and building up their winter home.

The grasshopper laughed at all the gathering, marching, and building. He couldn't think of anything sillier to do on a summer's day. It was a day for singing, so he sang and sang. Jumping was one of the grasshopper's favourite things, too, and he was very good at it. As a change from singing, he leaped through the grass, across the moss, and over the heads of the columns of busy ants.

He got tired of this before the ants did, because the ants never seemed to tire at all. Hundreds and thousands of them still marched through the forest. Pine needles, twigs, dry leaves, everything had to be carried to the anthill. The grasshopper heard their chants and made them into a song as they tramped past.

"Food for the queen! Ready for winter!" he sang, and giggled.

An ant stopped. "We all have to get ready for winter," he said. "Don't you have to collect food? Don't you need somewhere to keep warm when the frost comes?"

The grasshopper hadn't thought about this, and he laughed. Summer was no time to think about frost! He did a few jumps to show off, then sang another song and sang his way all through the summer.

When the anthill was warm and strongly built and the food stores were full, the weather grew colder and the days grew shorter. Winter crept frostily through the forest. The grasshopper huddled his wings together and shivered.

"I'm cold!" he said. His voice was low and weak. "And I'm so hungry!"

"Of course you are," said an ant hurrying to the safety of the anthill. "Why didn't you prepare for the winter instead of playing games and singing all day? Why didn't you make a food store and build a warm house?"

The grasshopper was too cold and too hungry to answer. He huddled up, shivering and empty, facing a harsh and bitter winter alone.

MAKE SURE YOU'RE PREPARED FOR HARD TIMES.

THE STAG AT THE POOL

D EEP IN THE FOREST, where sunlight filtered through the leaves and the streams wriggled quietly over stones, lived the deer. They were strong, graceful animals, tall glossy stags with branching antlers and proud, swift doe deer protecting their young, and all of them took care to stay in the secrecy of the trees. From time to time, men came riding into the forest with shrill hunting horns and fast, fierce dogs, ready to pull down a deer and kill it for meat, so the deer were shy and careful. Even in the heart of the forest they were always listening, alert for danger.

A tall and handsome stag came to a pool to drink, and as he drank he saw his reflection in the still water. When the ripples had settled, that reflection became very clear and he stepped back to observe it. He was pleased to see how much his antlers had grown in the last year.

"Those are magnificent antlers, though I say it myself!" he remarked. "They are stronger than ever before, and they've branched out at the top. I've never seen such antlers — they must be the best in the forest!" He turned his head from side to side to get a different view. "And that's a handsome head, too. It takes a well-shaped head to support a set of antlers like that."

He was becoming very glad he'd stopped at that pool. He was enjoying what it showed him and stepped a little closer.

"My coat is doing well this year, too," he observed. "It looks just as a good coat should, so it should be warm and thick in time for winter. But what... what are *those*?"

94

At first glance, he thought he was looking at four spindly little trees, young saplings with skinny trunks that looked as if they'd snap in a high wind. But as he looked, he realized with horror that they were…

"My *legs*! Oh, no! Those are…" – he was almost too appalled to say it – "my legs!"

Those legs were long and as thin as sticks with too-big, solid hooves and knobbly knees. The stag hung his head in shame, then glanced nervously from side to side hoping that there was nobody else there to see those long, thin, ugly legs. With any luck, an adult deer, whose eye level was about the same as his, would notice his antlers, not his legs – but what about the young animals? What about the foxes, the rabbits, the hares? The first thing they would see of him would be his legs, and he despaired at the thought of it.

Suddenly, from beyond the trees, came a sound that made the stag forget all about his reflection. It was the sound of a hunting horn, and soon after came the barking of dogs.

The stag turned and galloped further into the forest. Those long, slender legs carried him swiftly away over moss and stones, leaping over the streams and plunging into the shelter of the trees. Behind him, all the time, he could hear the hunting horns, the baying hounds, and the shouting voices, but no dog or horse could catch him.

With a sudden jerk of his head, the stag found that he was trapped. He tried to run, but his antlers were caught in the trailing branches of a tree and were so tangled that however much the stag strained and pulled, he could not free himself. The excited baying of the hounds was nearer, nearer, nearer. The trapped and terrified stag swung his head from side to side, strained, and struggled, but his handsome antlers held him fast. He was still there when the hunters found him. They killed him and carried home the body of the handsome stag with the slender legs and the proud antlers.

WHAT IS MOST IMPORTANT
MAY BE OVERLOOKED.

THE FOX AND THE GRAPES

WHEN FOX WAS just a little cub, his mother was very proud of him. She said he wasn't a fussy eater. "Bless his little heart," she said, "he'd eat whatever was put in front of him."

When he grew up, he still wasn't a fussy eater and he still ate whatever was in front of him. The only difference now was that he had to catch it first. He'd eat anything that couldn't run away fast enough. As Fox was quick on his paws and a sneaky thief, he helped himself to whatever he wanted – crunchy ducks and chickens, lamb, ham, salmon, gammon, and bread with jam on. If they'd had chips and dips in the forest, he would have eaten those, too, but they hadn't, so he didn't. In spite of eating so much, he was a lean, slinky fox, because most of his food had to be chased. He always had room for a little more.

One afternoon, he'd just eaten half a dozen raw eggs, a bread roll, and a weasel and fancied a bit of something sweet to finish

with. When he saw a bunch of green grapes hanging over a wall, he knew that they'd do very nicely. They were wet with rain, the sun was shining on them, and they looked *so* delicious. Fox licked his lips.

Unfortunately for Fox, the grapes were just a bit too far for him to reach in a single jump. (He found that out when he tried it.) He did his best to jump a bit higher, but he still couldn't reach those grapes, so he took a run at it. Still no good. He took a longer run, gathered himself up, jumped with all the power of every muscle in his long lean body, and snapped his jaws at those grapes, but his teeth clamped together on nothing and he landed with a thud. *Ouch.*

Jumping might not be the best idea, then. But didn't I tell you he was sneaky? He prowled along the bottom of the wall, trying to find a place where it was lower, so he could jump on, walk along it, and snatch the grapes. Sure enough, he came to a place where the wall had crumbled down, leaving a few bricks lying on the ground. Perfect. He scrambled on to the top of the wall. And fell off. The top of the wall was too narrow for a fully grown fox to walk along it.

Getting those grapes was turning out to be impossible, and Fox had an uncomfortable feeling that some other animals might be hiding in bushes, watching and giggling at him behind their paws.

Fox hated to be laughed at. He hated to fail, too. So, as he picked himself up and walked smoothly away, he remarked loudly, "There's a bunch of grapes on that wall, but I won't bother with them. They don't look that nice, so they're probably sour. Yes. Definitely sour!"

ANYONE CAN DESPISE
SOMETHING, JUST BECAUSE
THEY CAN'T HAVE IT.

THE LION, THE FOX,
AND THE BEASTS

HAVE YOU HEARD the news? The question was everywhere, passing around the forest. The goat said to the sheep, "Have you heard the news? The lion is dying!"

"Never! Who told you that?" asked the sheep.

"The lion says so himself," answered the goat. "He was so weak he could only crawl to the mouth of his cave and whisper that we should all go to see him. He's so noble, isn't he? He wants us to visit one at a time, so that he can say goodbye to each of us in turn. And he wants all of us to hear his last will and testament."

"What's a last — whatever it is?" asked the sheep. "Is it some sort of song?"

"You really don't understand much, do you?" replied the goat, who was very pleased to show off what he knew. "His last will and testament means his instructions for what to do with all his things after he dies. He'll tell us who's going to get his cave and who will be king after him, that sort of thing."

"I'm going straight there!" said the sheep, and away he went.

At the mouth of the cave lay a fox with its head on its paws. "Aren't you going in?" asked the sheep.

The fox looked down at the paw prints at the mouth of the cave. "I really don't think it's a good idea," he remarked, and yawned.

The sheep walked past him and into the cave.

A little later, having told all his friends about the lion's last will and testament, the goat arrived. The fox was still there with its

head on its paws and appeared to be asleep.

"Wake up, Fox!" said the goat. "We need to go in, to see the lion. We have to hear his will!"

The fox opened one eye. He looked down at the paw prints again. "Do you really think that's a good idea?" he asked.

"You'll miss your chance!" said the goat and he trotted into the cave. The fox appeared to go to sleep again.

It was some time later that the calf came past. The fox opened his eyes and stretched.

"The lion has sent for me," said the calf. "I have to go in! He wants to see me!"

"That really might not be a good idea, you know," said the fox. He sat up and looked down at the paw prints. "Perhaps you should turn around and go home."

"But it's what the lion says!" insisted the calf. "I can't keep him waiting!" and he trotted into the cave.

As the day wore on, the forest became quiet. No more animals came to the cave. The fox, hearing something moving in there, sat up straight, his ears lifted, his nose twitching, and the tip of his tail flicking from side to side.

The lion appeared at the entrance to the cave. He scowled at the fox.

"What are you doing there, you idle, disobedient fox?" growled the lion. "Don't you know I'm dying? Why haven't you come to me to pay your respects?"

"Your Majesty!" exclaimed the fox. "I'm delighted to see you looking so much better!" He took a few steps back. "But there are so many paw prints leading into your cave, and I can't see any coming out! So many have gone in, and so far, none of them have come out again. I did tell them it might not be a good idea."

Then he turned and ran, and kept running until he was safely home.

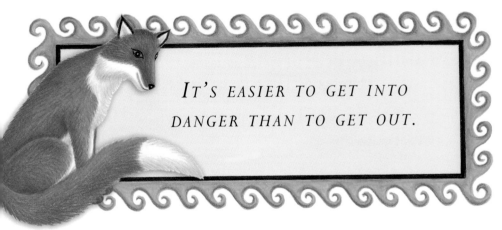

IT'S EASIER TO GET INTO
DANGER THAN TO GET OUT.

THE TOWN MOUSE AND THE COUNTRY MOUSE

EVERY DAY, CARTS rumbled from the town to the country and from the country to the town. From the country to the town they carried milk, cheese, butter, and vegetables, letters and parcels. The other way, they took pots and pans, bonnets, books, and even more letters and parcels. So if a town mouse wanted to go on a little trip, all it had to do was to jump on a cart. That's what Marcus Pinkear did when he went to the countryside to visit his cousin Joe.

At the farm gate, Marcus smoothed his glossy fur, took a deep breath of country air, and coughed, as he wasn't used to the smell of cowpats. He picked his way delicately down the farm track, carrying his long tail carefully over his arm, and found, near the edge of a field of yellow grain, a neat little shelter built of woven straw.

Marcus tapped at what looked like a door, but there was no answer, so he ducked to look through the gaps in the straw. Lying in the shelter, a plump little brown mouse lay on his back, his paws tucked in, holding his tail. He was snoring and looked very peaceful.

Marcus coughed politely. "Good afternoon, Joe," he said.

Joe stopped in the middle of a snore, shook himself, and woke up. "Wha–" he began, but when he saw his cousin, he jumped to his paws, threw his arms around him, and hugged him.

"Marcus!" he said. "How good of you to come! Are you well? You look as if you need some fresh country air! Tell me all about that place where you live! But not until you've had some refreshments after that long journey. Come in and rest, while I get you a drink and something good to eat."

"Oh… er… yes… right… thank you, thank you very much," stammered Marcus as Joe pottered away down the path. Marcus sat down and fanned himself with a feather. He was unpleasantly surprised. He hadn't remembered his cousin having such a rough coat, and there was a sheepy, earthy smell about him. In the town house where Marcus lived, you could always find a bit of soap if you knew where to look, and people left brushes and combs lying around. There was no excuse for looking scruffy. He reminded himself that he was in the country now and had to make the most of it, but all the same, he curled up his paws fastidiously. He'd rather not touch anything if he could help it.

There was a rustle in the grain stalks, and Joe appeared with his paws full.

"Here we are!" announced Joe. He put down two poppy petals to use as plates and spread out a meal – grain, blackberries from the hedge, and rainwater in acorn cups.

"This is all very – er – quaint," said Marcus. "It looks – er – exciting. But how do you live in winter? You can't survive out here!"

"No, I generally move into the old stables in winter," said Joe. "It's quite safe there. The cat doesn't bother exploring that far from the house, and the horses are friendly. There's plenty of food – they don't mind me sharing it. We live very simply here."

"Hmm," said Marcus, who didn't like the idea of drinking nothing but water all week. A drop of red wine would go down very nicely.

He spent a few days at Joe's house, but he found the shelter more and more uncomfortable and became sick of the sight of grain and blackberries. By the middle of the week, he was keen to get home and felt sure that Joe would be impressed by town life.

"It's my turn to offer you hospitality now," he suggested. "Come with me on the cart! Get a taste of town life! And I mean, taste! Roast potatoes! Jam! Croissants! Cakes!"

"I'm not sure," said Joe. "I suppose you're all very clever, educated mice in the city. You know all about table manners and things. I'd only show myself up."

"Nonsense, Joe!" said Marcus. "Nothing to worry about there. Please, please come."

So the two mice climbed onto the next cart and peeped over

the edge of a big round cheese as the cart jiggled toward the town. At first Joe was too nervous to speak, and after that he was too astonished.

Carts crowded the streets and the houses were crammed together with chimneys as high as the sky. There was rattling of wheels, barking of dogs, shouting of traders, banging of doors, and a clang-clung-ding of clocks chiming, doorbells ringing, and horseshoes on cobblestones. The ear-splitting ringing of a handbell made him duck behind the cheese.

"What was that?" he asked.

"It's only the school bell," said Marcus, who was enjoying the sights and sounds of the town again. "It means it's time for the children to come out of school."

"Do they have to warn the town that they're coming?" wondered Joe. When the cart jolted to a stop, the mice jumped down. It was a terrifying moment for Joe, who expected to be trodden on at any moment, but Marcus pulled him to a gap under a back door and through a hole at the bottom of the wall.

"We'll stay here for the moment," said Marcus, a bit out of breath. "It's best to hide until after dinner."

"Hide from what?" asked Joe, but Marcus didn't seem to hear. He was arranging wool and feathers into a nest.

"You look exhausted," he said. "Have a sleep before dinner."

Joe tried to sleep, but it took a long time to get all that noise out of his head, and the smells here were unfamiliar. There was paint and polish, and an animal smell that he knew he should recognize, but didn't. He fell asleep at last and woke when Marcus shook his shoulder.

"There's nobody in the kitchen!" said Marcus. "The family are all in bed. Time for a feast!"

Usually, Joe ate supper much earlier than this, and he felt hollow with hunger. He followed Marcus to the kitchen and they busily ate crumbs from the floor.

The bread was very good, but Marcus, who wanted to give Joe a treat, urged him to try a bit of everything. This wasn't what Joe was used to. Some of the cheeses were too strong and too strange, and the nuts had been covered in salt and spices. The cakes, jam, and cookies were far too sweet for a country mouse used to berries from the hedge, and he couldn't understand why anybody liked wine at all.

He did find some very good vegetables and was munching his way happily through the green beans when Marcus shouted, "Cat!"

Joe bolted for the nearest mouse hole, his mouth still full of beans. Marcus ran, too, and only just managed to whisk his tail in

before the cat's paws grabbed for it. Huddling against the wall, they saw the cat's nose as she sniffed left and right, and her sharp claws as she reached her paw into the hole.

"It's safe here," whispered Marcus. "She can't get in. She's always trying."

"Always!" thought Joe, wondering how often this had happened. A loud miaowing came from somewhere on the other side of the wall.

"That's the other cat," said Marcus. "Don't worry – she's a good mouser, but she's outside. Would you like to go to bed now?"

Joe spent a sleepless night. The rich food gave him a pain, the wine made his head ache, and the thought of those cats terrified him. At sunrise, he said goodbye to his cousin and was ready for the next cart home to the comforting smell, sight, and sound of cows and cornfields. He'd go on living on grain, berries, and water, but he wouldn't mind that at all.

BETTER PLAIN FOOD IN SAFETY
THAN A BANQUET IN DANGER.

THE GOOSE THAT LAID
THE GOLDEN EGGS

I F YOU WERE to go to Goosedown Cottage today, you'd find —
well, not much really. There are some tumbledown piles of stone
where the house used to be, but no sign of the vegetable patch or
the chicken shed. You can still see half a cowshed wall and a broken-
down gate where the goose pens were… oh, the goose pens!

Farmer Gaggle and his wife were both short and dumpy and just
a bit grumpy, and looked like a salt and pepper set. They grew food
in the little vegetable plot and sold the eggs from their chickens
and the milk from their cow. The farmhouse was small, but cosy
and warm, except when the roof leaked and Farmer Gaggle had to
patch it up. The food was a bit boring, but good enough and there
was plenty of it, and they could always look forward to starting the
day with a goose-egg omelette. Their best goose laid a big, warm

egg every morning, enough to make a delicious omelette for two.

One drizzly morning, when the sun was not quite up, Farmer Gaggle went down to the goose pens to fetch the egg. But underneath the goose there was no warm, smooth egg. There was something cold, hard, and heavy, and he muttered irritably as he slid it out from under the goose. He suspected that one of his neighbours might be playing a trick on him, putting a stone under his goose, and he was getting ready to be very huff-and-puff and angry about it. He stepped into the light with the hard, cold thing in his arms and dropped it, because it was so heavy.

"That can't be a goose egg," thought Farmer Gaggle, "because it didn't break. And because it shouldn't be that colour – and it shouldn't be that shiny…"

He picked it up again, very carefully, holding it up to the rising sun. He turned it around and saw how it gleamed in the early light. There could be no doubt about it. He held an egg of solid gold. Staggering, because it was heavy, he took it home to his wife. When she saw the shining egg, she forgot to be annoyed about missing her morning omelette. All Farmer and Mrs Gaggle could think of was how much money they could get for that egg. They went straight into town and sold it to a jeweller for more money than they had ever seen in their lives. They needed their wheelbarrow, first to carry the egg into town and again to take all their shopping home.

The next morning, the goose laid another golden egg. Farmer and Mrs Gaggle sold that one and bought winter clothes, summer clothes, boots, shoes, hats, and thirty-one pairs of socks each (one for each day of the month).

The morning after that, the goose laid a third golden egg. This time, the money paid for a carpenter to come and mend the roof.

Every morning, the goose laid another egg. Soon Farmer and Mrs Gaggle had a much smarter house, some more cows, dozens of chickens and geese, a flock of sheep, and a whole team of farm workers, shepherds, and milkmaids to do all the work for them. Oh, and a cook, a cleaner, and a gardener. And a horse and cart and a boy to run messages, so if they thought of anything else they wanted, they could send him on an errand. Then they did a few sums, got different answers, tried again, and worked out that after another thirty eggs, they could live very comfortably for the rest of their lives.

"It's a shame we have to wait so long for the eggs," said Mrs Gaggle with a sigh.

"A long time to go on living in this cranky old shed of a house and cleaning up after geese every morning," agreed Farmer Gaggle. They had become so used to getting whatever they wanted as soon as they wanted it that they had forgotten something very important. They had forgotten how to wait.

"That goose," said Mrs Gaggle. "All she ever gives us is one egg a day. I think she keeps us waiting on purpose."

"You could be right," said Farmer Gaggle. "She must be packed full of golden eggs."

Farmer Gaggle was not a clever man. Thinking wasn't his strong point. He took his axe, marched to the goose pens, caught the poor goose, and with one blow chopped off her head. Then he cut her down the middle and – yes, I'm afraid so – plunged his hands into the body.

There was nothing hard, smooth, or shiny in there. Not an egg, not a scrap or a fleck or a gleam of gold. He found only the warm, smelly, squishy insides of a goose.

Farmer and Mrs Gaggle never saw another golden egg for the rest of their lives. They lived grumpily ever after.

GREED DESTROYS EVERYTHING.

THE BOY WHO CRIED WOLF

THIS ISN'T A happy story. Are you ready?

His name was Jacob Herdwick Welsh, but everyone called him Jacob Sheep. He wasn't a sheep, he was a boy, and his job was to watch a flock of fifty sheep, feed them, and keep them safe. Believe me, it wasn't a lot of fun.

Lambs are great. They jump about, skip, run down hills just for the fun of it, and play King of the Castle on a rock, but when they grow up, they're just sheep. Mostly they're shaggy, stubborn, and slow (unless you've just rattled a bucket of turnips at them, and then they charge like a herd of wild elephants and knock you over). Apart from that, they eat, bleat, and sleep. Now and again one would run off and try to jump over the fence and Jacob would have to chase it back, but that was the most exciting thing that ever happened. The sheep were really important to the people in the village, who depended on them for meat and wool,

but they were still boring animals. In case the flock was ever attacked by a wolf, Jacob had a stick – and a whistle to blow so that people would come running to help, which was just as well, because a stick wouldn't be much use against a hungry wolf.

Sometimes Jacob thought it would be great if the sheep were attacked by a wolf. It would be a change from counting the silly beasts and chasing them away from the fence. Then he had an idea that he thought was brilliant. Unfortunately, it wasn't. It really, really wasn't.

He thought it would be fun to blow his whistle, yell "WOLF!", and see what happened. The more he thought about it, the more he wanted to do it, until one morning...

"WOLF!" shouted Jacob. He filled his lungs, blew that whistle with all his might, and shouted again, "HELP! WOOOOOLF!"

Suddenly, everyone was running to the sheep field. Red-faced farmers with spades and pitchforks, old men shaking their sticks, grannies brandishing their knitting needles, everyone left their work and ran to chase away the wolf. Jacob doubled over and laughed until his legs gave way, and he rolled on the grass having hiccups.

Nobody else laughed. The farmers, old men, and grannies, and all the other people, who were all out of breath, couldn't see anything funny about it at all, and were grumbling and annoyed as they plodded away. Unfortunately, Jacob still thought it was funny. He thought it was so hilariously funny that he did it again a week later. Again, everyone came running to help, and this time, they were even angrier as they stormed away. Jacob just laughed.

One morning, when he rattled the bucket of turnips at the sheep, they didn't gallop toward him and knock him over. They all ran the other way and stood huddling together in a corner, shaking and staring at something behind him. Jacob looked round to see what it was.

"WOLF!" shouted Jacob — because there it was, with its huge red mouth, its long sharp teeth, its fierce eyes, and its tongue licking its lips as it prowled toward him. He blew his whistle so hard that his lungs hurt and shouted again, "HELP! WOLF! WOLF, WOLF, WOOOOOLF!"

Everybody heard him. Nobody came. The farmers, old men,

grannies, and everybody else only shrugged and muttered that young Jacob was at it again. When somebody finally did go to the sheep field, they saw some very frightened sheep, but not as many as there should be. They found Jacob's shoes, his stick, and his whistle. He'd never cry "wolf" again.

I told you it wasn't a happy story.

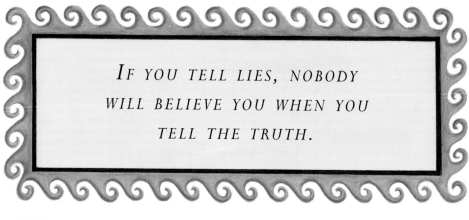

IF YOU TELL LIES, NOBODY WILL BELIEVE YOU WHEN YOU TELL THE TRUTH.

AESOP AND ME

Aesop lived about two and a half thousand years ago in Ancient Greece, in an age that loved learning. Like a lot of people, he was full of advice about how to live your life. What made Aesop different was the way he made everything into stories, especially animal stories that are good to read and act, and easy to remember, and have their grain of teaching as well. That's why ever since Aesop's time, storytellers have told and retold them, written and rewritten them. When it was time for me to try, I began with a good look at the collection. That made for some surprises.

The first surprise was how many stories there are! There are so many of them, it wasn't so much "what do I put in?" but "what do I leave out?" In the end, I chose some of the best-loved stories and my own favourites. I found "The Silkworm and the Spider" and "The Clown and the Countryman", which were new to me, and I liked them a lot.

The next surprise was working my way through a list of Aesop's stories and thinking, "Oh, now I know where that comes from!" There were some very familiar old tales in there, but I'd never known that they were from Aesop's fables. I remember reading the story of "The North Wind and the Sun" in a book at school. I loved that one and remembered it all my life, but I only just discovered that it's one of Aesop's. So is "The Goose That Laid the Golden Eggs".

There are all kinds here – some have happy endings, some don't. Some, like "The Father and His Daughters", don't really give you an ending, but leave you asking yourself a question. They all have morals to teach, but some of them are funny. Because Aesop's fables are so old, people can be very solemn and stuffy about them, but "Belling the Cat" tickled my funny bone, so I wrote it as a funny story. And the same goes for that well-known old tale, "The Hare and the Tortoise".

Reading and rereading the stories, I found that Aesop was talking about a harsh world. These stories are full of warnings. *Be wary.* These forests are full of cunning animals who can't be trusted ("The Lion, the Fox, and the Beasts"). *Be honest.* Nobody respects a liar ("The Monkey and the Dolphin"). On the other hand, they may not believe the truth ("The Clown and the Countryman"). *Take care to be ready for hard times* ("The Ant and the Grasshopper"). Life is easier now than it was in ancient Greece, but those lessons are still worth knowing. Take care, be honest, prepare for the future – but, as that poor milkmaid would tell you, don't think so much about the future that you don't notice what's going on in the present. (By the way, I feel really sorry for that poor grasshopper. Why couldn't those goody-goody ants have taken him in and looked after him?)

There are happier truths in Aesop, too, about friendship and loyalty. There's "The Lion and the Mouse" and "Androcles and the Lion". Do you know people who bore you to death going on about their hobbies, their music, or where they went on holiday? I think Aesop must have known people like that, because he told the story of "The Town Mouse and the Country Mouse". It's there to remind us that what suits you might not suit somebody else.

There's another truth, a very important truth, that Aesop understood very well. It's one of the most important lessons in the world, and you will find it in the story of "The Lion and the Mouse". This story tells you that *you* count, *you* matter, *you* can do great things. You may be small. You may think you're not very good or not much use – but listen to the story. You can make a difference. There may be something that only you can do. The world needs you.

And, finally…

AUNT ISA'S BOOKSHELF

COME WITH ME. Come to a dark, old-fashioned living room from long before you were born. It is a dark Sunday evening. Apart from the pale flowery wallpaper, everything seems to be in different shades of brown. The armchairs, the settee, and the home-made hearthrug are well worn. Oil paintings hang on the walls. A small television with a rounded screen and buttons is in a corner, but as usual, it's switched off. The lights are dim. There is an electric fire, which looks as if it's coal but isn't really, and a tall lamp with a fringed lampshade.

In the room the grown-ups are talking, as grown-ups do (apart from the old man who has fallen asleep and snores occasionally). There are two elderly ladies, the aunts: Aunt Evie, who is tiny, like a little hobbit with thick glasses, and her tall sister, Aunt Isa, who has a loud voice. A married couple sit on the settee; the woman is knitting — *click, click, count the stitches, click, click, click*.

There are two daughters, and the grown-up talk is nothing to do with them. The older girl, Helen, is curled up in a corner, reading. I don't know what she's reading, but she is well organized and probably brought a book with her.

On a leather footstool beside an armchair sits a fair-haired child wearing a tartan skirt, a hand-knitted sweater, and long white socks. This is Margaret. The leather of the footstool sticks to the backs of her legs and stings when she moves, and she is bending over a book. Maybe she forgot to bring her library book with her, or perhaps she's finished it, but she hasn't got anything with her to read. She has looked on her aunts' bookshelf and found a book of Aesop's fables, so she's reading that, but the print is tiny, the light is low, and, to be honest, the stories are written very plainly. Whoever wrote these down didn't try to make them fun. There are no pictures at all, not even black and white line drawings. She is thinking, "They don't seem like stories. I'm sure I could make them more exciting than this."

I hope I have done that at last. And here, instead of plain printed pages, you have the skilled and breathtaking pictures by Amanda Hall, full of bright fur and very much alive animals. Here you are in the bright, colourful, and glowing world of Aesop's fables!

And look out for wolves.

Please note that no mice, monkeys, or aunts were harmed in the making of this book.

Margaret
x